night Creatures

By Kathryn Stevens

The
Child's
World®
www.childsworld.com

Published in the United States of America by The Child's World®
1980 Lookout Drive • Mankato, MN 56003-1705
800-599-READ • www.childsworld.com

ACKNOWLEDGMENTS

The Child's World®: Mary Berendes, Publishing Director

Produced by Shoreline Publishing Group LLC
President / Editorial Director: James Buckley, Jr.
Designer: Tom Carling, carlingdesign.com
Cover Design: Slimfilms

Photo Credits
Cover–Minden Pictures (main); iStock (insets)
Interior–Corbis: 23; Dreamstime.com: 5, 6, 8, 9, 10, 11, 12, 14, 15, 18, 26, 27, 29; iStock: 15, 19, 21, 24; Photos.com: 7, 17, 24.

LIBRARY OF CONGRESS CATALOG-IN-PUBLICATION DATA

Stevens, Kathryn, 1954–
  Night creatures / by Kathryn Stevens.
    p. cm. — (Reading rocks!)
  Includes bibliographical references and index.
  ISBN-13: 978-1-59296-855-8 (library bound : alk. paper)
  ISBN-10: 1-59296-855-4 (library bound : alk. paper)
 1. Nocturnal animals—Juvenile literature. I. Title. II. Series.

QL755.5.S89 2007
591.5'18—dc22

2007011416

CONTENTS

WHILE YOU'RE
Sleeping

You've said good-night. You're tucked under the covers. The light is out. You're ready for a good night's sleep. Everything is dark. Everything is quiet and still . . . or is it?

Some animals don't go to bed when you do! All around you, they're creeping, crawling, and slithering. They're flying, burrowing, walking, and swimming. Some of them are trying to stay safe. Others are on the prowl, hunting and killing. There's a whole living world out there that we

rarely get to see! It's an amazing world that scurries on in the dark while you're safe in your bed. It's the world of **nocturnal** animals—the creatures of the night.

This Eurasian eagle owl is nocturnal. Its big eyes help it to see well in the dark.

5

What does it take to live at night? You need to be able to find your way around in the dark. You need to find food and shelter and watch out for danger. If you're a **predator**, you need to be able to hunt.

Lots of daytime animals have **camouflage** (KA-muh-flazh), coloring that helps them hide. But many night animals have protective coloring, too. An owl's splotchy feathers, the stripes on a raccoon's tail, and a jaguar's spots all act as camouflage. They break up the animals' colors. They help the animals blend in

This photo of an owl's feathers shows how it might blend into a tree's branches.

with light and shadows. Camouflage helps the animals stay safe—or sneak up on their **prey**.

Lots of nocturnal animals see really well in the dark. They often have big eyes—like the owl's eyes on page 5. Big eyes allow more light to get in. The **pupils** of many nocturnal animals aren't round like ours. Some are slits instead. At night, the slits open wide to let in lots of light. In bright light, the slits close almost shut to protect the eyes.

A jaguar's spots help it hide amid shady jungle trees.

7

Fennecs have the biggest ears of any fox. They look huge against the animal's small body.

Many animals use their sense of smell to find their way in the dark. Raccoons have an outstanding sense of smell. They can find food even in the middle of the night. Deer and rabbits use their sense of smell to stay safe from predators, find food, and communicate with each other.

Lots of night animals can hear really well. Some have big ears that pick up lots of sounds. Fennec and kit foxes live in desert areas. Their big ears help them get rid of extra body heat. They also help the foxes hear and find small animals to eat.

You can't see owls' ears very well because they're covered with feathers. But these nocturnal hunters have some of the best hearing in the world. The feathers on their faces form a "dish" to funnel sound to their ears.

A horned owl gets its name from the feathers that stick out on its head. The feathers are not just decoration— they help the owl hear better.

On many owls, one ear is higher than the other. This helps the owl tell whether a sound is coming from high or low, or near or far. In fact, the owl can hear exactly where to find its prey. Sometimes owls can even hear prey moving under the snow!

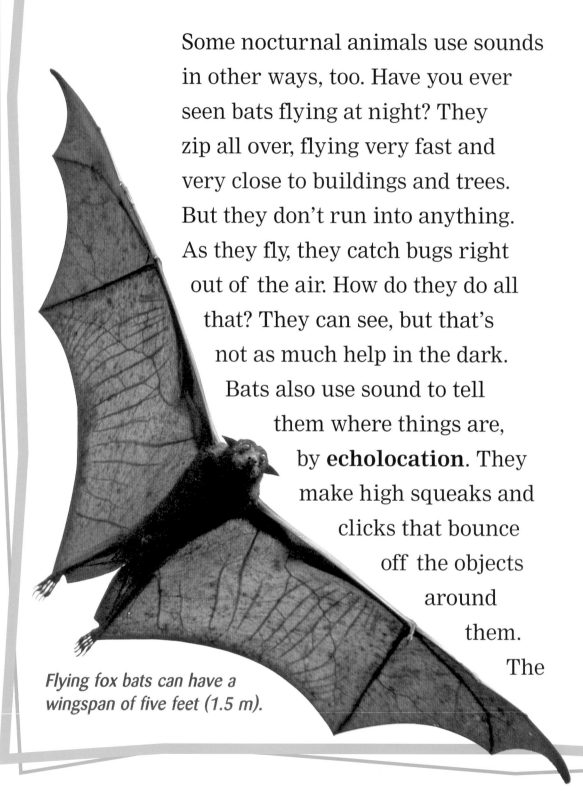

Some nocturnal animals use sounds in other ways, too. Have you ever seen bats flying at night? They zip all over, flying very fast and very close to buildings and trees. But they don't run into anything. As they fly, they catch bugs right out of the air. How do they do all that? They can see, but that's not as much help in the dark. Bats also use sound to tell them where things are, by **echolocation**. They make high squeaks and clicks that bounce off the objects around them. The

Flying fox bats can have a wingspan of five feet (1.5 m).

sounds come back as echoes. The echoes tell the bats where things are, and what sizes and shapes they are. Bats "see" their nighttime world through sound!

Snake tongues pull in lots of information about the world around them.

Some nocturnal animals can feel or even taste their way around. Snakes' tongues taste the water, the air, and the ground. The snakes use their tongues to help them find and track prey, avoid predators, or find other snakes. Moths and other insects have feelers, or **antennae** (an-TEH-nee). The antennae help the bugs smell, taste, and feel the world around them.

2

In YOUR OWN
Backyard

An amazing number of animals are nocturnal—even in your own backyard.

In warm weather, you can hear the nighttime sounds of chirping crickets and croaking frogs. Mice rustle through dead leaves on the ground. Moths flutter around plants and lights. Raccoons hunt for food, sometimes in garbage cans. Deer munch on tender shoots and the corn in farmers' fields. Birds and bats zip through the skies.

OPPOSITE PAGE
Raccoons are experts at finding food, even from inside garbage cans.

Lots of small animals stay safer by living nocturnal lives. Many beetles and other bugs are nocturnal. Living at night helps them avoid daytime predators such as birds.

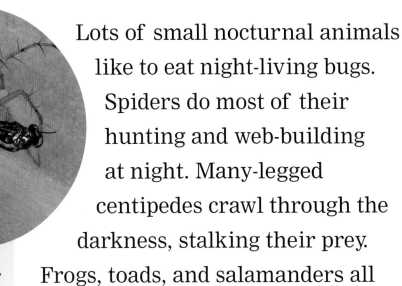

A lynx spider wraps up a fly to eat later.

Lots of small nocturnal animals like to eat night-living bugs. Spiders do most of their hunting and web-building at night. Many-legged centipedes crawl through the darkness, stalking their prey. Frogs, toads, and salamanders all hunt bugs and grubs at night, too.

Some birds also hunt bugs at night. Nightjars are nocturnal birds that love to eat bugs. Nighthawks

Going Batty for Bugs!

Some kinds of bats eat fruits or fish or even blood. But most North American bats eat bugs—and more bugs. Many bats can eat half their weight in bugs every night! The little brown bat can eat up to 600 mosquitoes in an hour!

are one kind of North American nightjar. They fly around at night, snagging bugs right out of the air. Scientists found more than 500 mosquitoes in one nighthawk's stomach! Nighthawks don't have long, hard beaks. They have big, soft mouths with whisker-like feathers. The feathers act like a funnel to help them scoop up their prey.

This nightjar blends in with the dusky night sky as well as leaves in the trees.

What other little animals come out at night? Mice. Many, many mice! Mice come out at night to eat and to try to stay safe. There are lots of other animals that want to eat them. Mice are an important food for owls, hawks, foxes, and many other predators.

Even at night, tiny mice have to be careful to look for predators.

Foxes also are active at night. They hunt mice and other small animals. They even eat smaller critters such as worms, grubs, and beetles. Coyotes often do their hunting at night, too. In many places, you can hear them yipping and howling in the darkness. They have great senses of sight, smell, and hearing. Those senses help them hunt

An adult coyote is about the same size as a small collie dog.

Foxes and coyotes have adapted fairly well to living around people. Sometimes people see them even in big cities.

mice and other small animals, as well as deer. Coyotes even find and eat **carrion**—the meat of dead animals. In some areas, nighttime howling comes from another kind of hunter—wolves! Packs of wolves working together can hunt larger animals such as deer, elk, moose, and even cattle.

A raccoon's hands can do almost as many things as our hands.

One nocturnal animal doesn't really try to hide. A skunk's bold black-and-white coloring warns animals and people—stay away! If skunks are scared or upset, they spray musk that has a horrible smell.

If you're talking about backyard animals, you can't forget those "masked bandits," raccoons! Raccoons sometimes appear during the day, but they're especially active at night. They're very smart. They've learned to live in all kinds of places—from forests and farms to the middle of big cities. You can find raccoons stealing corn or just eating from a garbage can.

Opossums come out at night, too. These strange-looking animals are North America's only **marsupial.** Like koalas and kangaroos, opossums keep their babies safe inside a pouch on their bodies.

Opossums climb trees really well. They can even hang from their tails! They shuffle around at night looking for all kinds of food, from berries and bugs to people's garbage.

Beavers are also especially busy at night! That's when they build and repair their dams.

Marsupials are animals that carry and feed their live young in a pouch on their body.

Opossums are easily spotted by their gray fur and pink noses.

Other **mammals** are active at night. In eastern North America, you sometimes see white-tailed deer during the day. But as the sun goes down, the deer come out to eat. You see them feeding in farmers' fields or along the roadside.

Bears are active at night, too. Many parts of North America have black bears or brown bears. Both kinds

nocturnal...People?!

While you're snoozing at night, lots of people are working. They have jobs that can't wait for daylight. Doctors and nurses work all night to take care of sick and injured people. Police officers, firefighters, soldiers, and security guards keep people and property safe. Pilots and other airline workers fly people from place to place. Factory workers make all kinds of things, from soda pop to cars. These are just a few important nighttime jobs.

Black bears usually live in wooded areas, but they come out to look for food.

Flying squirrels are an unusual nocturnal animal. They don't really fly, but they glide really well. Big flaps of skin between their front and back legs stretch to form "wings." These "wings" let them soar from tree to tree.

eat lots of different foods, including berries, fish, bugs, and small animals. In some places bears look for food at the town dump at night. Campers have to be careful not to leave food around overnight! Clever bears can break into coolers, tents, and even cars to steal tasty treats.

3

NIGHT IN THE Big World

Other parts of the world have nocturnal bugs, bats, and birds that are pretty much like ours. But they also have some very different night animals!

Walkingsticks are amazing nocturnal insects. The bodies of these plant-eating bugs look just like the twigs and leaves on which they live. Walkingsticks' lives depend on their camouflage. During the day, these insects hardly move— although they might sway a little. That makes them look like branches blowing in the breeze.

New Zealand's kiwi is an odd-looking bird. It's famous for not being able to fly. But did you know it's also nocturnal? It prowls around looking for worms, bugs, seeds, and berries. Kiwis have long beaks and good senses of smell. They snuffle around in the dirt, looking for dinner.

Kiwis can smell well because, unlike most birds, their nostrils are near the end of their beaks.

Have you ever heard of lorises, bush babies, pottos, lemurs, and tarsiers? These big-eyed creatures are related to monkeys. They live in trees and are active at night.

Lorises live in Asia and creep around slowly, eating fruit, bugs, and other small animals. Galagos are small lorises that live in Africa, where they jump from tree to tree. They're often called "bush babies" because their cry sounds like a human baby. Pottos live in Africa, too. They curl up in a ball during the day. At night they hunt for fruit, eggs, and bugs.

When leaping from tree to tree, bush babies use their long tails to help steer.

Lemurs live only on the island

Here is a good look at the huge eyes of a tree-dwelling tarsier.

The owl monkey is the only kind of true monkey that's nocturnal. Owl monkeys live in the rain forests of Central and South America. At night, they eat fruit, insects, and small animals.

of Madagascar. One type is called an aye-aye (EYE-eye). They listen for grubs inside trees. Then they rip open the tree with their teeth and dig out the grubs. Rat-sized tarsiers live in Asia and eat bugs and lizards. Tarsiers' eyes are huge—even for nocturnal animals!

The Tasmanian devil looks like a large, black rat.

You might know Tasmanian devils from cartoons. But they're real creatures, too! These odd nocturnal animals live only in Tasmania, an island near Australia. Like opossums, they're marsupials. They roam around at night, sniffing out carrion to eat. Sometimes they hunt small, live animals, too.

How did they get their name? Because they make loud, creepy sounds in the dead of night. They scream, screech, snarl, and growl—especially when they're feeding. People thought they sounded like devils.

North America isn't the only place where bears come out at night. Sun bears are small bears that live in Southeast Asia. They got their name from big yellowish markings on their chests. At night they look for food—anything from insects and small animals to fruit. They even crack open big, hard coconuts! Their long tongues help them scoop up honey and insects.

Sun bears use their tongue like a long spoon to reach into insect nests.

South America also has a type of nocturnal bear. Spectacled bears live in the Andes Mountains. Rings of lighter fur around their eyes look like eyeglasses, or spectacles.

Many of the world's big, wild cats are nighttime hunters. Jaguars are huge, spotted cats that live in Central and South America. They grow up to 6 feet (almost 2 m) long and can weigh as much as 300 pounds (136 kg). The only cats that are bigger are lions and tigers. Jaguars roam around at night, stalking their prey. They swim and climb very well. They pounce on animals of all sizes, from fish and turtles to wild pigs and even cattle.

Clouded leopards live in the rain forests of Southeast Asia. They get their name from their cloudy-looking spots. Clouded leopards can open their mouths very, very wide. And they have really big teeth!

Lions usually hunt at night, when it's cooler. They hunt either alone or in groups. During the day, they rest in the shade.

Their pointy fangs are 2 inches (5 cm) long. That's the same size as tigers' teeth—but tigers are 10 times larger!

This jaguar is resting up for a long night of hunting.

Far away or close to home, there's more to the natural world than we see with our own eyes. The next time you tuck yourself into bed, remember—there's a whole world of animals just starting their "day"!

GLOSSARY

antennae movable feelers on the heads of insects and some other animals that help them find out about their surroundings

camouflage special coloring or markings that help an animal blend in with its surroundings

carrion the rotting meat of dead animals

echolocation a way in which some animals find and identify nearby objects by sending out sounds and listing to the echoes

mammal an animal that has fur, gives birth to live young, and feeds its young milk

marsupial an animal that carries its young in a pouch of skin

nocturnal active mostly at night

predator an animal that hunts and kills other animals for food

prey animals that other animals hunt as food

pupil the dark opening that lets light into an animal's eye

FIND OUT MORE

BOOKS

The Night Book, Exploring Nature after Dark with Activities, Experiments and Information
Pamela Hickman. (Kids Can Press, 1999)
Find fun things to do in this hands-on book about nighttime creatures of all kinds.

Night Science for Kids, Exploring the World After Dark
*Terry Krautwurst. (*Lark Books, 2003)
Check out the activities and inside-science stories in this fact-filled book.

Vampire Bats and Other Creatures of the Night
Philip Steele. (Kingfisher, 1995)
A close-up look at the most famous nighttime creatures of all.

WEB SITES

Visit our Web page for lots of links about animals who come out at night: www.childsworld.com/links

Note to Parents, Teachers, and Librarians: We routinely check our Web links to make sure they're safe, active sites—so encourage your readers to check them out!

INDEX

KATHRYN STEVENS is an archaeologist as well as an editor and author of numerous children's books on nature and science, geography, and other topics. She lives in western Wisconsin, where she spends her spare time enjoying the outdoors, restoring a Victorian house, and making pet-therapy visits with her dog.